CAVING

BY SARA GREEN

BELLWETHER MEDIA • MINNEAPOLIS, MN

Jump into the cockpit and take flight with Pilot books. Your journey will take you on high-energy adventures as you learn about all that is wild, weird, fascinating, and fun!

This edition first published in 2014 by Bellwether Media, Inc.

No part of this publication may be reproduced in whole or in part without written permission of the publisher. For information regarding permission, write to Bellwether Media, Inc., Attention: Permissions Department, 5357 Penn Avenue South, Minneapolis, MN 55419.

Library of Congress Cataloging-in-Publication Data

Green, Sara, 1964-
 Caving / by Sara Green.
   pages cm. – (Pilot: Outdoor Adventures)
 Includes bibliographical references and index.
 Summary: "Engaging images accompany information about caving. The combination of high-interest subject matter and narrative text is intended for students in grades 3 through 7"– Provided by publisher.
 ISBN 978-1-62617-084-1 (hardcover : alk. paper)
 1. Caving–Juvenile literature. I. Title.
 GV200.62.G73 2014
 796.52'5–dc23

                                        2013034260

TABLE OF CONTENTS

AN UNDERGROUND ADVENTURE

A group of cavers peers into a dark opening on the side of a hill. It is the entrance to a cave. A map of the cave shows an underground passageway that leads to a large room. The cavers are excited to see what they will find there. Once the group steps inside, the light from the cave's entrance quickly fades. Soon, they are in complete darkness. The only light comes from headlamps mounted on their helmets.

The passageway is narrow and the ceiling is low. The cavers must crouch as they walk. Suddenly, they arrive at a wall. The path continues through a small opening near the ground. One by one, the cavers crawl through the hole on their bellies. On the other side is a vast chamber. A waterfall splashes into a crystal clear pool. Stalactites hang from the ceiling. Stalagmites rise from the cave's floor. The cavers are astounded to find such wonders underground!

Caving is an activity where people explore natural underground areas called caves. Caves are plentiful, and many remain undiscovered. People explore caves to experience the fascinating world beneath the surface of the earth. Many seek to discover and map new territory. Cavers also enjoy pursuing new challenges. They navigate deep pits and narrow corridors to test their courage.

Spelunkers

Spelunking is another word for caving. Many people use the term *spelunker* for people who have little caving experience. Those with more experience are called cavers.

Some cavers are speleologists. These scientists explore caves to learn how they were formed. Rocks provide clues about the ancient geology of the earth. Speleologists examine insects and other animals to learn how they survive in the dark. Artifacts tell them about humans who lived in the caves long ago. Scientists also use the information they collect to teach others how to preserve these unique places.

Most people explore caves formed in limestone rock. They are made by rainwater dripping onto the limestone. This process breaks down the rock and leaves small cracks that enlarge over time to form hollow spaces. These spaces join together to become underground rooms and passageways big enough for cavers to investigate. Inside, a caver moves through three zones. The entrance zone has some light, and the twilight zone has little light. The dark zone has no light at all.

Cavers spend most of their time exploring the dark zone. With their headlamps, cavers observe spiky stalagmites and stalactites. Other rock formations are named for their appearance. Soda straws, cave bacon, and cave pearls are a few of these. Some caves have walls of sparkling crystals. Lucky cavers may encounter underground lakes or waterfalls.

cave
bacon

cave
popcorn

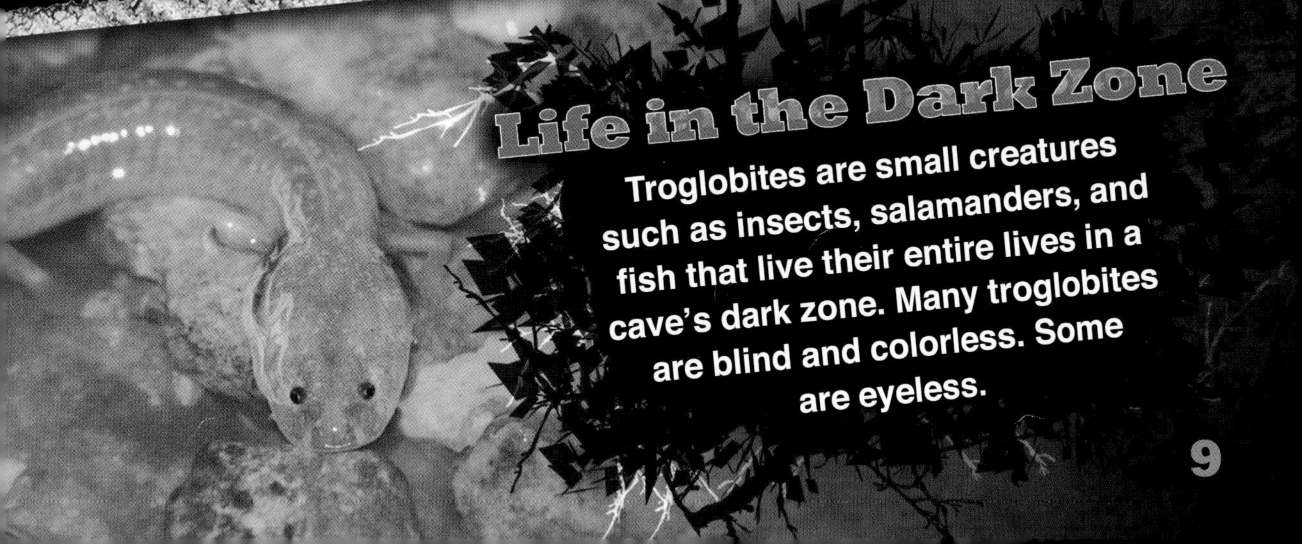

Life in the Dark Zone

Troglobites are small creatures such as insects, salamanders, and fish that live their entire lives in a cave's dark zone. Many troglobites are blind and colorless. Some are eyeless.

Limestone caves come in various shapes and sizes. Some are barely large enough for two people. Others contain rooms big enough to hold a crowd. Most cavers prefer to explore horizontal caves. The passageways of these caves are mostly on one level. The longest caves twist and turn for hundreds of miles underground. Horizontal caves are often filled with obstacles. Cavers may have to squeeze through narrow openings on their hands and knees. Some may have to wade through deep pools of water.

Other cavers enjoy the challenges of vertical caves. These caves require skills similar to mountain climbing. Cavers use ropes and cables to descend into deep pits to reach the floor of a cave. They must also be able to climb back out. Vertical cavers learn special knots and climbing skills to stay safe. They spend hours practicing outside of caves. Many vertical cavers practice on ropes hanging from trees!

11

Some types of caves are found in unexpected places. Lava tubes are made from lava flow. Hot lava moving through a shell of cooled lava creates tubes where people can walk. Sea caves are formed by waves pounding against rocky cliffs. Cavers often approach these from the water. They paddle through the caves using kayaks. Much of the time, lava tubes and sea caves can be explored by people with little caving experience.

hardened lava

Some people explore caves hidden deep underwater in oceans, rivers, and lakes. These cave divers have advanced scuba diving and underwater skills. Because cave diving is so dangerous, only the most expert divers should attempt it. Most divers train for several years before they are ready to explore underwater caves. Their efforts pay off when they see the mysterious beauty of an underwater cave for the first time.

GEARING UP TO EXPLORE

Cavers must be prepared to handle dark, dirty, and dangerous conditions. Helmets protect cavers' heads from falling rocks and low ceilings. Headlamps on helmets provide the main source of light and allow cavers to keep their hands free. Cavers must also bring a spare headlamp, a small flashlight, and extra batteries. Cavers exploring vertical caves need ropes, harnesses, and other gear designed for climbing in caves. All cavers should bring first-aid kits, extra food, and water.

harness

Each cave is different. Cavers should dress for a cave's conditions. Many dress in layers of warm, lightweight clothes that can get wet and dirty. Some wear waterproof overalls as a top layer. Gloves keep hands warm and dry. Cavers should wear sturdy boots to walk on muddy, slippery rock. Many cavers also wear kneepads for crawling on rocks.

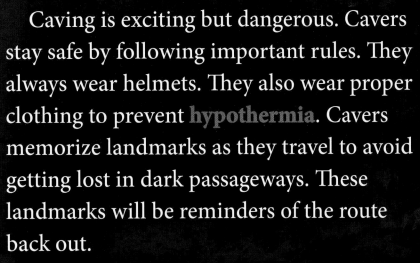

Caving is exciting but dangerous. Cavers stay safe by following important rules. They always wear helmets. They also wear proper clothing to prevent hypothermia. Cavers memorize landmarks as they travel to avoid getting lost in dark passageways. These landmarks will be reminders of the route back out.

Cavers should never explore a cave on a rainy day. Rainwater can trap cavers in an unexpected flood. If a cave begins to fill with water, cavers should seek high ground. There, they must wait for water levels to lower before leaving the cave. Cavers should always explore in groups of four or more. If an injury occurs, one person stays with the injured caver while the others go for help. Someone outside the group should know the cave's location and the group's return time. This person can bring help in an emergency.

PROTECTING CAVES

Cave environments are fragile. Most caves take thousands of years or more to form. Cavers must take care to protect them. Rock formations can be damaged when people touch them. Plants and animals can be harmed or killed when people **pollute** their habitat. People who put **graffiti** on cave walls leave scars that may never go away.

A Long Process

Most limestone caves need at least 100,000 years to become large enough for people to move around inside.

Responsible cavers respect nature. They never leave a trace of their visits in caves. Rocks, crystals, and animals are left undisturbed. All leftover food and trash is taken home. Many caves are on private property. Cavers must ask permission from landowners to explore these caves. Landowners often close caves permanently if too many people enter without permission. Some caves are closed during parts of the year to protect bats. Others are closed because of safety concerns. No matter the reason, responsible cavers never enter closed caves.

MAMMOTH CAVE

Beneath the hills of Kentucky lies Mammoth Cave, the world's longest known cave. So far, explorers have mapped 400 miles (644 kilometers) of passageways. Mammoth Cave has at least five levels that descend 379 feet (116 meters) below the surface. They include huge rooms, deep shafts, and fantastic rock formations. Underground rivers plunge into waterfalls. The lowest levels are often completely submerged in water. More than 130 kinds of animals live in the cave. Twelve of these are eyeless!

Mammoth Cave National Park offers visitors the chance to experience the cave. Park rangers lead tourists on guided hikes across 14 miles (23 kilometers) of trails. Many visitors prefer easy strolls on lighted walkways. Those seeking a challenge can go on a Wild Cave Tour. Here, people brave the dark to crawl through tight spaces and hike steep underground trails. These cavers get the thrill of exploring places most people will never see!

Show Caves

In show caves, guides lead people on well-lit, marked walkways. Visitors do not need special gear to experience cave sights.

Kentucky

N
W   E
S

Mammoth Cave

GLOSSARY

artifacts—objects made by humans long ago; artifacts tell people today about people from the past.

descend—to go down

geology—the study of rocks, minerals, and other physical properties of the earth

graffiti—words or pictures carved or drawn on cave walls or formations

harnesses—safety belts with leg loops

horizontal caves—caves that are mostly on one level

hypothermia—dangerously low body temperature

lava tubes—caves made by flowing lava; lava is hot, melted rock that flows out of an active volcano.

limestone—a type of rock made from the shells of sea creatures

pollute—to make a natural area dirty and unsafe for living

sea caves—caves made by waves hitting cliffs repeatedly

speleologists—scientists who study caves

stalactites—rock formations that hang from a cave's ceiling

stalagmites—rock formations that build up from a cave's floor

tourists—people who travel to visit another place

vertical caves—caves that have shafts and pits

TO LEARN MORE

At the Library

Champion, Neil. *Wild Underground: Cave and Caving Adventure.*
Mankato, Minn.: Black Rabbit Books, 2012.

David, Jack. *Caving.* Minneapolis, Minn.: Bellwether Media, 2009.

Sisk, Maeve. *Caving.* New York, N.Y.: Gareth Stevens Pub., 2013.

On the Web

Learning more about caving
is as easy as 1, 2, 3.

1. Go to www.factsurfer.com.

2. Enter "caving" into the search box.

3. Click the "Surf" button and you will see a list
of related Web sites.

With factsurfer.com, finding more information
is just a click away.

INDEX

The images in this book are reproduced through the courtesy of: William Storage/ Getty Images, front cover, pp. 16-17; Robbie Shone/ SuperStock/ Getty Images, pp. 4-5, 6-7; Chris Howes/ Wild Places Photography/ Alamy, p. 9 (top left); salajean, pp. 9 (top right), 19; Matt Jeppson, p. 9 (bottom); Stephen Alvarez/ Getty Images, pp. 10-11; Photononstop/ SuperStock, pp. 12, 15; age fotostock/ SuperStock, p. 13; Design Pics/ SuperStock, p. 14; Robin Loznak/ AP Images, p. 18; National Park Service/ Wikipedia, p. 21.